GR E
Po

MW00980655

Women Inventors

2

Amanda Jones, Mary Anderson,
Bette Nesmith Graham, Dr. Ruth Benerito,
Becky Schroeder

by Jean F. Blashfield

Capstone Press

MINNEAPOLIS

Printed in the United States of America.

Capstone Press • 2440 Fernbrook Lane • Minneapolis, MN 55447

Editorial Director   John Coughlan
Managing Editor   Tom Streissguth
Production Editor   James Stapleton
Book Design   Timothy Halldin
Picture Researcher   Athena Angelos

Library of Congress Cataloging-in-Publication Data

Blashfield, Jean F.
    Women inventors / by Jean F. Blashfield.
      p.   cm. -- (Capstone short biographies)
    Includes bibliographical references and index.
    Summary: Each volume presents brief accounts of five women and their inventions.
    ISBN 1-56065-275-6
    1. Women inventors--United States--Biography--Juvenile literature. 2. Inventions--United States--History--Juvenile literature. [1. Inventors. 2. Inventions. 3. Women--Biography.] I. Title. II. Series.
    T39.B53   1996
    609.2'273--dc20   95-442
    [B]   CIP
                                                                       AC

Table of Contents

AMANDA T. JONES

TAKEN IN 1872, JUST BEFORE THE WRITING OF THE CRUSADE DOCUMENTS.
CLIFTON SPRINGS, N. Y.

Amanda Jones
1835-1914
Patents for Preserving Food

As she lay in her bed, trying to get well, Amanda Jones never felt sorry for herself. Her mind was busy. She wrote poetry. She made up stories. And she thought about practical things. She wanted to invent things to make life easier for people.

Amanda Theodosia Jones was born in East Bloomfield, New York, in 1835. She was the fourth of the 12 children in her family. Bright and interested in everything around her, she started teaching at the age of 15.

Amanda had health problems that bothered her all her life. She spent long periods of time in bed, where she began to write poetry.

After Amanda moved to Chicago, she worked as an editor, preparing magazines for printing. Throughout her life, Amanda Jones worked at writing. But she also developed another interest–inventing.

The Inventor at Work

In 1872, Amanda had an idea for a way to preserve fresh food by putting it in sealed glass

Amanda Jones created a system for removing air from glass jars. This prevented food spoilage.

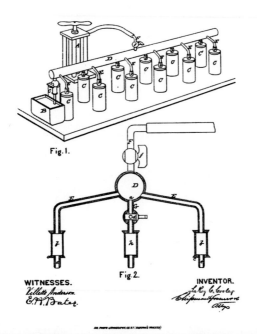

Mason jars have been used for many years to preserve fruits and vegetables.

jars. This way of preserving food, called **canning**, had already existed for several decades. No one knew why it worked. It was not until 1860 that Louis Pasteur of Paris, France, proved that mold and bacteria cause food to spoil. Canning protected food from mold and bacteria.

Amanda Jones's method of canning called for air to be sucked out of the canning jar. This created an airless space, or **vacuum**. The air was replaced with very hot liquid and the jar was immediately sealed. She worked out the method for the Jones Process with her cousin, Professor Cooley of Albany, New York. The U.S. Patent Office granted Amanda and the professor five different patents for canning in 1873.

After a brief effort to start a company to vacuum-can foods, Amanda went back to writing.

The Spirit Healers

In the late 1800s, **spiritualism** was very popular. This was the belief that certain people, called mediums, have the power to communicate with the spirits of dead people. Amanda Jones believed that she was a medium. She said that a spirit told her to work on inventing an oil-burning heater. At that time, people were just discovering how useful petroleum oil could be.

In 1880, Amanda patented a room heater that burned oil as its fuel. During the following

A Psychic Autobiography

BY

AMANDA T. JONES

Author of "ULAH," "ATLANTIS," "POEMS," (of the Rebellion)
"A PRAIRIE IDYL," "RUBAIYAT OF SOLOMON," "POEMS;
1854-1906," ETC.

With Introduction by JAMES H. HYSLOP, Ph. D., LL. D., Secretary of the American Society for Psychical Research

*Drink waters out of thine own cistern and running
waters out of thine own well.
Let thy fountains be dispersed abroad and rivers
of waters in the streets.*
                                    —*Proverbs V; 15, 16*

**Amanda Jones wrote of her experiences
as a medium who communicated with
the spirit world.**

years, she acquired three more oil-heater patents.

Amanda returned to food processing in 1890, when she started the U.S. Women's Canning and Preserving Company of Chicago. Only women worked there and shared in the ownership of the company. It lasted until 1921.

Before she died in 1914, the inventive Amanda Theodosia Jones had obtained 12 patents.

Mary Anderson
1866-1953
The Real Inventor of the Windshield Wiper

A visitor from Alabama was riding the streetcar through the streets of New York City. Through the window she was enjoying the sight of the city's crowded streets in a snowstorm. Fascinated, she gazed at the tall buildings, the noisy horseless carriages, and the people.

Streetcars had to run every day, and in all kinds of weather.

Then her attention was caught by something inside the streetcar. The motorman who was running the streetcar was getting very cold. In order to watch the traffic and the pedestrians, he had to keep snow from covering the front window. Every few minutes, he had to reach through an opening in the glass to wipe the snow off the windshield.

Mary Anderson tried to think of a way for the motorman to stay warm while clearing the window. Ignoring the sights around her, she sketched in her mind a solution to the problem.

A Southern Lady

Mary Anderson was born in Alabama in 1866. In that warm southern state, it rarely snows. So when Mary was visiting New York City, snow was new to her. The problem of the shivering motorman was also new.

When she returned to Alabama, she thought more about the shivering motorman working hundreds of miles away. Gradually she worked out the details of the solution that had come to her on the streetcar.

Mary's plan called for a long scraping arm to be attached to the outside of the window. Its handle would be on the inside. The motorman could turn the handle and move the scraper blade back and forth. It would make a fan-shaped, clear space on the glass. The motorman would get the window clear, but he would not get his hand icy.

A One-Time Experience

Mary's friends laughed at her invention, but she applied for a patent anyway. She was granted a patent for the idea in 1903. (An illustration of the patent can be found on page 35.)

Mary Anderon tried to sell the rights to her idea, knowing that cars, trucks, and streetcars could all benefit from it. She sent it to only one company, and they rejected it.

Mary packed away her papers. She did not try again to sell the rights to her patent. In fact,

Most early automobiles were open cars and were not equipped with widshield wipers.

she even forgot about the idea. Eventually, her patent lapsed and the law allowed somebody else to copy it. Mary Anderson never invented anything else and she died in 1953.

Writers of later years credited a man with the invention of the mechanical windshield wiper in 1916. They did not know that a woman had already created it many years before.

Bette Nesmith Graham
1924-1980
Hiding Her Mistakes

Bette Claire McMurray was not a good typist. In fact, she made a lot of mistakes. But that didn't stop her from becoming an inventor and a millionaire. She did it by finding a way to cover up her typing errors. Secretaries everywhere liked her idea.

Bette was born in Dallas, Texas, in 1924. She dropped out of high school to go to work when World War II started. Her employers, impressed by her ability, paid for her to go to a school for secretaries. She learned many useful skills but did not become a skilled typist.

In the days before computers, typists had to be very, very careful. Otherwise, the letters they typed would look messy. They often had to make more than one copy of a letter. To make copies, they used black carbon paper, which transferred the typed letters to a second sheet of paper. Fixing a mistake when using carbon paper was even messier.

A Typist's Self-Defense

After World War II, Bette Nesmith divorced her husband and went to work as a secretary in a bank. Bette still had trouble with her typing and spent a lot of time trying to make neat corrections. One day, she brought some white paint from home and used it to cover a mistake. She then typed in the correct letter over the

At one time, nearly everyone who typed had a small bottle of Liquid Paper handy to cover mistakes.

white paint. This method kept her from having to re-type many letters.

Other secretaries in the bank asked to borrow her paint. She decided to sell it. Working in her kitchen at night, she experimented with many different kinds of paint. When she found just the right one, she put it in tiny bottles and sold it as Mistake Out.

Bette turned her garage into a small factory. Her son Michael, who would later join a popular singing group called the Monkees, helped her bottle Mistake Out. She built a small building in her backyard and hired some employees. She worked to improve the special white liquid, patented it, and changed its name to Liquid Paper. She also began to offer colored liquid to cover mistakes on paper of different colors.

Tiny Bottles Make Music

Bette Nesmith became Bette Nesmith Graham when she married again in 1964. Her Liquid Paper had become popular all over the world, and her company was international. The Gillette Company eventually bought it from Bette for almost $50 million.

By that time, Bette had stopped working for the company. She was using the money she had earned from her idea to work with many charities and churches.

Dr. Ruth Benerito
1916-
Changing the Nature of Nature

Have you ever seen cotton sheets taken from the washing machine? During the wash, they become wrinkled. People used to iron sheets and pillowcases so they would be smooth when they were put on a bed. Cotton clothing also wrinkled badly. Blouses, skirts, shirts, and pants all had to be ironed before they could be worn.

In the late 1930s, a chemical company, E.I. du Pont de Nemours and Company, invented a **synthetic**, or laboratory-made, **textile** called nylon. Other kinds of synthetic fabrics, such as polyester and Acrilan, later appeared on the market.

These synthetics were popular because clothing made of them did not require much work. They did not get as dirty as cotton. When washed, they dried quickly and without wrinkling badly. People called these fabrics wash-and-wear, or drip-dry.

But synthetic fabrics also made people feel hot. And synthetic shirts and pants often had a shiny look that many people did not like. Also, these fabrics were made out of chemicals drawn from petroleum, a **nonrenewable resource**.

The falling sales of cotton clothing harmed southern farmers, who were selling less of their cotton crop. Many people wanted to go back to wearing cotton because it was comfortable. They wished cotton were as easy to take care of as synthetics. A textile chemist named Dr. Ruth Benerito gave these people what they wanted.

Helping Agriculture

Ruth Rogan Benerito was born in New Orleans, Louisiana. She earned a college degree in chemistry from Newcomb College and a higher degree from Tulane University. After she taught high school chemistry for awhile, she earned her highest degree, a Ph.D., from the University of Chicago in 1948. When she married, Dr. Ruth Rogan became Dr. Ruth Benerito.

Dr. Benerito went to work in the laboratories of the U.S. Department of Agriculture (USDA). The USDA wanted to help cotton farmers start selling their cotton again. In order to get people

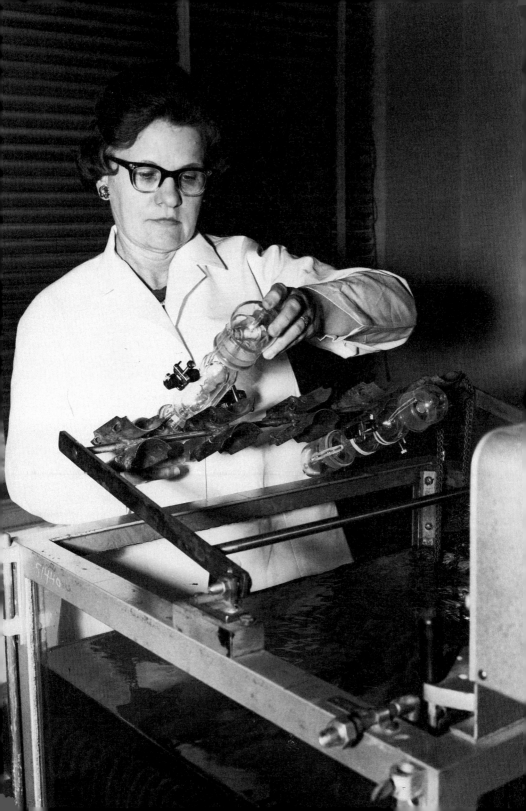

to buy cotton clothing, cotton would have to be made as easy to care for as synthetic fabrics. It would have to be even better than nature had made it.

The Long-Lasting Task

In order for Dr. Benerito to solve the problem, she had to understand the chemistry of cotton. She had to know what chemicals are in it, and how these chemicals work together to form **fibers**. She had to know how the fibers absorb liquids and how liquids dry from them.

For more than 10 years, Dr. Benerito worked on changing the chemistry of cotton to help it resist wrinkling, whether it is wet or dry. Along the way, she found ways to make it stop absorbing oil and water. She did it by inventing new chemical **compounds** that change the

Dr. Benerito spent 10 years in a research laboratory to develop a wrinkle-free cotton.

nature of cotton. Over the years, the Patent Office granted her more than 50 patents for these new compounds.

Dr. Benerito did not work only on textiles. She also made important discoveries on the way fat is used in the body and how it can affect heart disease. She was the winner of many awards from the U.S. government and from the chemical industry. In 1971, she was named one of the most important women in the United States by the *Ladies' Home Journal*.

Becky Schroeder
1962-
Turning Up the Light

Becky Schroeder was born in Toledo, Ohio, in 1962. Like many children, she often sat in the car while her mother ran errands. One late afternoon, she was doing her fifth-grade homework in the car. It gradually got darker and darker, until she could no longer see. She found herself wishing for something that would help her keep writing.

Wishing Wasn't Enough

While she waited for her mother, she started thinking. Perhaps she could use **phosphorescent** chemicals, which give off a light of their own. When she got home, Becky asked her father, a lawyer, for some of these chemicals.

Becky mixed several of these phosphorescent chemicals together. Using a special plastic board, she found she could draw lines on the board that would glow through a sheet of paper. Her invention, called the Glo-Sheet, helps people write in a straight line even when little or no light is available.

Getting a Patent

Becky already knew about inventions and patents. Her father is a lawyer who helps people get patents. He helped Becky get a patent for her Glo-Sheet.

In her patent application, Becky described different uses for her invention. In hospitals, doctors who visit patients at night could write without turning on a light. Pilots who take notes while they fly at night could leave the

The Glo-Sheet allows writers to work without light.

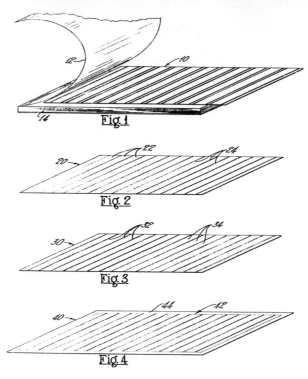

The patent drawing for Becky Schroeder's Glo-Sheet shows a simple and clever design.

lights off in the cockpit. And children waiting for their mothers in dark cars could do their homework.

When her patent was granted, Becky, then 12 years old, received a lot of publicity. She told *Seventeen* magazine that her patent did not affect her private life. "My friends were just very surprised," she told the reporter.

Continuing to Improve

Becky knew that many patents are granted to people for improvements to earlier patents.

The Glo-Sheet can be very practical for restaurant patrons.

She worked on improving her own invention. Now that she could write in the dark, she wanted to read in the dark, too. She came up with a way to make a menu that could be read in a dark restaurant. She also invented a new kind of Glo-Sheet strip that could be moved up and down behind a sheet of paper.

For the next 10 years, Becky continued to make improvements on her Glo-Sheets. She applied for an additional patent each time. When she was in her 20s, she started a company called B. J. Products Inc. to manufacture several different versions of her Glo-Sheet.

Instead of just thinking, "I wish I could see to write straight in the dark," Becky Schroeder did something about the problem. She believes that many young people could become inventors if they would just take their own ideas seriously.

More about Inventing

In 1790, the new U.S. Congress passed a law that gave people the right to stop others from copying their inventions. This law, called patent law, allows men and women to protect their inventions.

The first woman to take advantage of the law was Mary Dixon Kies of Killingly, Connecticut. In 1809, she patented a device to weave thread and straw into bonnets and hats.

Women may have invented other things in the years between 1790 and 1809. But some states did not allow married women to own property, and a patent counts as property. A woman's patent had to be in her husband's name.

Today, the government still grants most patents to men. But the number of women getting patents in their own names is rising. So, too, are the number of children getting patents. Anyone can apply for a patent, as long as the idea is original.

What to Do with a Good Idea

You may have a bright idea for a new or improved product. You need to know how it

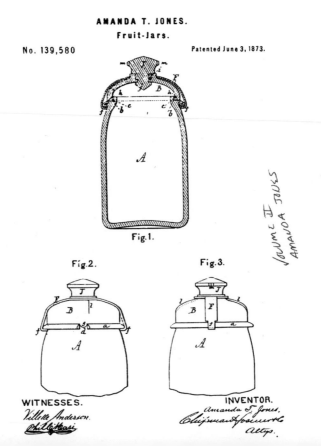

AMANDA T. JONES.
Fruit-Jars.

No. 139,580

Patented June 3, 1873.

Fig.1.

Fig.2.

Fig.3.

WITNESSES.
Villette Anderson.

INVENTOR.
Amanda T. Jones.
attys.

can be produced. You also have to figure out what claims you can make for it. Are all of its parts new? What is it good for? Just how useful is it?

Many people have a lawyer help them find out whether anything about their invention is already protected by another patent. The lawyer can help an inventor file the right papers for a patent.

For more information on the details of obtaining a patent, write:

Office of Information
U.S. Patent Office
Washington, D.C. 20231

or:

Canadian Intellectual Property Office
Industry Canada
Place du Portage, Phase I
50 Victoria Street
Hull, Quebec K1A 0C9
Canada

Children Inventing Things

Children have invented many useful things. Some have invented toys and games. When Hannah Cannon of Hollywood Hills, California, was in the eighth grade, she invented a card game. It is a word game a little like Scrabble, but it is easier to carry around. Called Cardz, the game sold in bookstores all over the country.

Young Inventors Today

The Westinghouse Science Talent Search is a program for high school students. Science-minded students do research, write a paper, and take a difficult examination. The winners receive college scholarships.

In 1995, the second-place winner invented something very important. Tracy Phillips of Long Island, New York, invented an electronic wallet that identifies paper money for blind

Mary Anderson was unable to sell her windshield wiper. Eventually the patent lapsed, allowing someone else to copy it and profit from it.

WINDOW CLEANING DEVICE.

APPLICATION FILED JUNE 18, 1903.

NO MODEL.

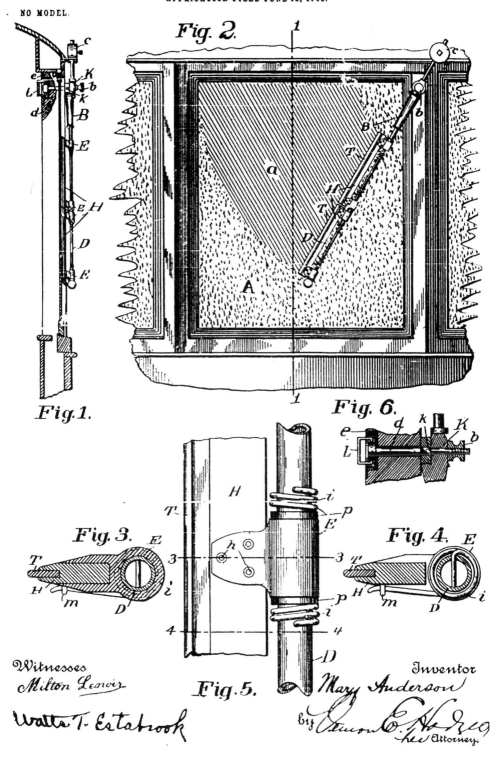

Fig. 2.

Fig. 1.

Fig. 6.

Fig. 3.

Fig. 5.

Fig. 4.

Witnesses
Milton Lenoir
Watts T. Estabrook

Inventor
Mary Anderson
by Vernon E. Hodges
her Attorney.

people. She created a portable light detector that reads whether a bill is $1, $5, or $10. The amount is sent to an electronic voice chip that tells the blind person what bill it is.

Tracy received a $30,000 scholarship to attend Massachusetts Institute of Technology. She is very proud to help people who cannot see.

Invent America!

The U.S. Patent Model Foundation is trying to find and preserve models of patented items made in the 19th century. They are also trying to make sure that Americans invent new things in the 21st century.

Invent America! is a program to encourage elementary school students to think creatively. Each year since 1984, students have submitted their inventions. They go to Washington, D.C., to vie for prizes in a national competition.

Some of the inventions created by elementary school children are unusual. One is pet food served with an edible spoon, so the pet owner does not have to wash the spoon. Another is a disposable shield to protect a painter's hand from a drippy paint brush.

Margaret Knight's bag machine was the first to assemble flat-bottom grocery bags.

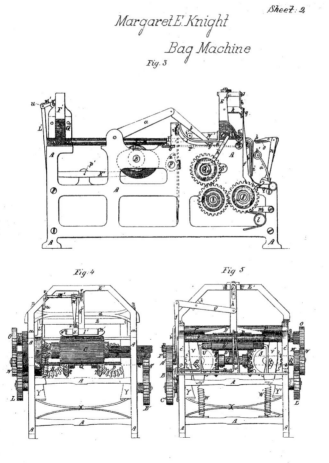

Glossary

canning–the preservation of food by sealing it in specially prepared and heated jars or tin cans.

compound–a substance made out of several different chemical elements. Many compounds are found in nature, but chemists can make new ones to do special tasks.

fiber–a long, very thin strand. Cotton fibers are spun together to make thread.

nonrenewable resource–material from the earth that cannot be grown again once it is used up. Plants are the only truly renewable resource.

phosphorescent–describes a substance that can glow without an outside source of light.

spiritualism–the belief that the spirits of the dead can be contacted by certain people, called mediums

synthetic–describes a substance made in a laboratory, and which is not found in nature

textile–cloth of any kind. Originally, "textile" meant just woven cloth.

vacuum–a space that is completely empty, where even the air has been removed

To Learn More

Aaseng, Nathan. *Twentieth-Century Inventors.* New York: Facts on File, 1991.

Bundles, A'Lelia Perry. *Madam C.J. Walker.* New York: Chelsea House Publishers, 1991.

Epstein, Vivian Sheldon. *History of Women in Science for Young People.* Denver, Colo.: VSE Publishers, 1994.

James, Portia P. *The Real McCoy: African-American Invention and Innovation, 1619-1930.* Washington, D.C.: Smithsonian Institution, 1989.

Lafferty, Peter. *The Inventor Through History.* New York: Thompson Learning, 1993.

Macaulay, David. *The Way Things Work.* Boston: Houghton Mifflin, 1988.

McKissack, Patricia and McKissack, Fredrick. *African-American Inventors.* Brookfield, Conn.: The Millbrook Press, 1994.

Pizer, Vernon. *Shortchanged by History: America's Neglected Innovators.* New York: Putnam, 1979.

Richardson, Robert O. *The Weird and Wondrous World of Patents.* New York: Sterling Publishing, 1990.

Showell, Ellen and Amram, Fred M.B. *From Indian Corn to Outer Space: Women Invent in America.* Peterborough, N.H.: Cobblestone Publishing, 1995.

Sproule, Anna. *New Ideas in Industry: Women History Makers.* New York: Hampstead Press, 1988.

Vare, Ethlie Ann and Ptacek, Greg. *Women Inventors and Their Discoveries.* Minneapolis: The Oliver Press, 1993.

Veglahn, Nancy. *Women Scientists.* New York: Facts on File, 1991.

Weiss, Harvey. *How to Be an Inventor.* New York: Thomas Y. Crowell, 1980.

Yenne, Bill. *100 Inventions That Shaped World History.* San Francisco: Bluewood Books, 1993.

You can read articles about women inventors in the June 1994 issue of *Cobblestone: The History Magazine for Young People.*

Places to Visit

Inventure Place: National Inventors Hall of Fame
221 S. Broadway
Akron, OH 44308

California Museum of Science and Industry
700 State Drive
Los Angeles, CA 90037

Franklin Institute Science Museum and Planetarium
20th and Benjamin Franklin Parkway
Philadelphia, PA 19103

Lawrence Hall of Science
University of California
Centennial Drive
Berkeley, CA 94720

Museum of Science
Science Park
Boston, MA 02114

Museum of Science and Industry
57th Street and Lake Shore Drive
Chicago, IL 60637

National Air and Space Museum
Sixth and Independence Avenue S.W.
Washington, DC 20560

National Museum of American History
24th Street and Constitution Avenue N.W.
Washington, DC 20560

Some Useful Addresses

Affiliated Inventors Foundation
2132 E. Bijou St.
Colorado Springs, CO 80909-5950

Invent America!
510 King St. Suite 420
Alexandria, VA 22314

Inventors Clubs of America
Box 450261
Atlanta, GA 30345

**Inventors Workshop International
  Education Foundation**
7332 Mason Ave.
Canoga Park, CA 91306

National Inventors Foundation
345 W. Cypress St.
Glendale, CA 91204

National Women's History Project
7738 Bell Road
Windsor, CA 95492

Society of Women Engineers
120 Wall St., 11th Floor
New York, NY 10005

The Women Inventors Project
1 Greensboro Drive, Suite 302
Etobicoke, Ontario M9W 1C8
Canada

A Summer Camp for Young Inventors

Hands-on activities in science, technology, and the arts are offered at Camp Invention, a weeklong summer camp held at various sites throughout the United States. The camps, sponsored by The National Inventors Hall of Fame, are for students in grades one through five. A companion program, Camp Ingenuity, was recently launched for students in grades six through eight. For information, call 1-800-968-4332.

Index